Héloïse Pajadou's Calvary

I0540832

Lucien Descaves

Translated By Richard Robinson

Sunny Lou Publishing Company
Portland, Oregon, USA
http://www.sunnyloupublishing.com

1st Edition Corrected, 13 July 2021

ISBN: 978-1-955392-07-5

* * *

This translation from French is based on
the Henry Kistemaeckers' publication of *Le Calvaire de
Héloïse Pajadou,* Paris, 1883.

Contents

Foreword

Sed ut perspiciatis, unde omnis iste natus error sit voluptatem accusantium doloremque laudantium, totam rem aperiam eaque ipsa, quae ab illo inventore veritatis et quasi architecto beatae vitae dicta sunt, explicabo. Nemo enim ipsam voluptatem, quia voluptas sit, aspernatur aut odit aut fugit, sed quia consequuntur magni dolores eos, qui ratione voluptatem sequi nesciunt, neque porro quisquam est, qui dolorem ipsum, quia dolor sit, amet, consectetur, adipisci velit, sed quia non numquam eius modi tempora incidunt, ut labore et dolore magnam aliquam quaerat voluptatem. Ut enim ad minima veniam, quis nostrum exercitationemullam corporis suscipit laboriosam, nisi ut aliquid ex ea commodi consequatur? Quis autem vel eum iure reprehenderit, qui in ea voluptate velit esse, quam nihil molestiae consequatur, vel illum, qui dolorem eum fugiat, quo voluptas nulla pariatur? [33] At vero eos et accusamus et iusto odio dignissimos ducimus, qui blanditiis praesentium voluptatum deleniti atque corrupti, quos dolores et quas molestias excepturi sint, obcaecati cupiditate non provident, similique sunt in culpa, qui officia deserunt mollitia animi, id est laborum et dolorum fuga. Et harum quidem rerum facilis est et expedita distinctio. Nam libero tempore, cum soluta nobis est eligendi optio, cumque nihil impedit, quo minus id, quod maxime placeat, facere possimus, omnis voluptas assumenda est, omnis dolor repellendus. Temporibus autem quibusdam et aut officiis debitis aut rerum necessitatibus saepe eveniet, ut et voluptates repudiandae sint et molestiae non recusandae. Itaque earum rerum hic tenetur a sapiente delectus, ut aut reiciendis voluptatibus maiores alias consequatur aut perferendis doloribus asperiores repellat.

– Cicero, 45 BC (*de Finibus Bonorum et Malorum*)

Héloïse Pajadou's Calvary

I

He pursued her for a week, whispered in her ear behind doors, waited for her huddled in the back corners of the laundry room. The first day she worked there he wanted her. Her naked arms, very white, aroused him. But the girl, who let him kiss her wrists and the nape of her neck, stubbornly refused to let him kiss her lips. While crossing a hallway, brusquely, she felt him snatch at her boldly and uncover her breasts. "No!" she cried and always succeeded in disengaging herself, either by slipping through his fingers, or because Mother Vaillant, ever watchful, placed her overweight body and searching eyes between her son-in-law and the female worker.

Finally, Pajadou lost his patience. He had to have her or he was not a man! So he waited for her, one evening, in a room where they piled up the linen, before wringing it, and where the women dolled themselves up before exiting.

Léotine arrived, listless and tired. Little drops

of sweat, the size of the head of a needle, glistened on her neck.

Pajadou grabbed hold of her by her wrists. She, not in the least surprised that he was there, looked at him coldly, but with a recoil of all her body.

"I want you," he said, imperatively this time.

A stubborn determination darted out from his eyes: "You understand! I'm the boss, I can sack you. 's no shortage of workers who'd ask for nothing better than to work here! Two refused me... the twits! They cleared off, it didn't take long!"

As he spoke with the girl, he coveted her slatternly flesh, with her thick hair, drenched in sweat, and he desired her something fierce in spite of her imperfections: her nose was too long, the lips too thick, with dark gaps between her teeth. Her cheeks, beneath glaucous eyes, were blotched by very vivid red freckles on drab pale skin.

Pajadou seized her. She grew faint, collapsed under his brutal thrust, her back buried, lost in the linen.

Night was falling; the room was filled with undulating moans of growing intensity, and the shadows of bundles, stacked higgledy-piggledy in the room, were etched on the wall like the silhouettes of enormous bellies.

After a minute, Mother Vaillant was on the doorsill, her eyes squinting, trying to see in the darkness.

Pajadou saw his mother-in-law and, immediately calmed down, without the humility of a schoolboy caught in the act, walked passed her and exited, desirous of avoiding a scene, leaving the fat woman disconcerted by such audacity.

But she had her revenge soon enough. Two slaps rang out, and Léotine filed out, followed by shoves and crude phrases.

Having chased the girl out, Mother Vaillant stopped, totally shaken, her fists on her hips. A hesitation seized her. Should she tell her daughter about the incident? "No," she concluded, "that fool, Héloïse, would eat her heart out!"

Pajadou, from a window on the second floor, silently laughing to himself, watched Léontine, planted in the middle of the courtyard, patting her skirts down and playing with her crupper like a wet dog after a downpour.

II

Héloïse Vaillant had married Pajadou one year after the death of her father, who owned with his wife a laundry in Cachan. The wife and daughter had quickly understood that they could not run the business alone, with all its incumbent responsibilities; the presence of a man in the home was indispensable.

As the clientele was excellent and the Vaillant family's financial position was likely to continue to improve, suitors for Héloïse's hand in marriage were not lacking. But the young lady surprised everyone, and her mother more than anyone, by choosing a boy employed at the laundry, Etienne Pajadou. He was thirteen years older than his wife, not handsome, and had a reputation in the town for being an incorrigible skirt chaser. For sure, he had bewitched that twenty-year-old, brown-haired beauty, with her very long and sweet dark eyes, her ample chest, her fresh face of a chaste virgin. People continued to ask themselves for a long time afterwards how he had done it, on that occasion, that bawdy fellow who boasted that he had never "given a fuck about women" and that he had possessed them all with little to no effort on his part. Those prompt capitulations had surprised everyone who knew the man. Such was he on the day of his marriage, and that is pretty much how Héloïse found him after ten years of cohabitation. Squat, with short legs, but of medium height, his length being all in the torso, he had a bull's neck, strong shoulders, and, in spite of a torpid appearance, great muscular strength.

Marriage, a regular life, had accentuated his body's thickening-out, which his features were naturally inclined to. Now his entire face presented a purplish bloatedness and his cheeks, enlarged, made his eyes look smaller to the point that they seemed like two blue-gray, shining bars. His thin sideburns were turning gray, as well as the hair on his head, and his lips, carefully shaven, above and below, were thick and wet, and had frothy slaver at the each corner, something that people with prognathous jaws are sometimes afflicted with.

In the space of five years, Pajadou had four

children with his wife. Those were, despite the fatigues of maternity, the best years of Héloïse's married life.

Caught off guard by an unexpected turn of good fortune, Pajadou, his initial drunkenness dissipated, coldly examined his situation. He hadn't entered into the laundry business on an equal footing, and only noticed it after several days. Mother Vaillant appeared determined in disputing his position, and she rode roughshod over him by virtue of her prior authority, which she had no intention of abdicating. This big woman, very active, very restless in spite of her round haunches and her large breasts, would have preferred to subject, than accept, her son-in-law. A man was needed around the house, that was indisputable, but she still would have liked to have chosen a malleable and tender pate, someone disposed to a slow incubation.

He would have been her thing, her aide, an aide whom she appointed with misgiving and whom, alone, events would have imposed on her.

From the start, Pajadou and his mother-in-law were irreconcilable enemies; only Pajadou, like a guest who arrives late, dissimulated, observed, was circumspect. He realized that the boss lady would not let herself be circumvented easily, and he made himself ingratiating, effaced himself with a sly guile. For goodness sake! he knew quite well that Mother Vaillant would never accept him flat out, so it was the entourage instead, his wife at first, the workers, and then the neighbors that he endeavored to gain favor with.

He affected not so much the airs of a loud-farting parvenu, but a syrupy and tenacious good-naturedness that disarmed people. He labored liked a simple worker, but desirous above all that everyone got into the habit of going to him when they had questions or concerns, he went so far as to deliver fresh linen to the clients, every Monday.

His wife was immediately taken in by him; he had an ineluctable ascendent over her, which was supposed to tip the balance in his favor in the probable case of a discussion with his mother-in-law. Little by little, without fuss, without fanfare, he played his hand perfectly. Now everyone was on his side: a fellow so gentle and so obliging: incapable of harming a fly! Even the stories of his chasing skirts were abandoned like fastidious old news.

But it was at the conclusion of Héloïse's last pregnancies when he truly set himself up at the laundry. He was called the boss, and Mother Vaillant's authority was definitively reduced. She was nothing more now than the old boss, a loudmouth whose exterior was in sharp contrast to the unctuous mellifluousness of her son-in-law.

She didn't admit defeat. Her mute rancor, nourished on griefs too vague to bring up, waited merely for an occasion for her to re-affirm herself peremptorily. To the compliments that benign people made about Pajadou, Mother Vaillant responded with dubious nods of the head. To several intimate acquaintances she confided even that she had proof that the sugary appearance was just proud Jesuitism. Besides, one would see!

Her reserve of earlier days gave way to a hateful distrust, instinctively. Common interests brought them together, nothing more; the questions and answers, like well-tempered sharp blades, made sharp, clear, chinking sounds; their mouths exhaled coldness and bitterness.

Mother Vaillant had more than one screw to turn! She had been, in fact, the mistress of the laundry for ten years; she had worn the pants in the enterprise, swallowed her husband whole, commanded, bent the personnel to her will, and now an intruder was wheedling his way in with bright ideas of improvements, plans of reform, at the core of which was to use vapor more widely and adopt of a new model of wringers.

The laundress fell back on her daughter, in the hope that she would furnish her with material for reproaches, motives for hatred. Héloïse remained silent with a gentle sadness, which could not even be taken for resignation.

Her four successive labors had exhausted her, prematurely aged her. The croup had taken away her two oldest children, and it was a miracle that she had nearly escaped a peritonitis that her last two deliveries brought on.

She came out of that illness thin and pale, her cheeks faded, her bosom flattened, her back curved with a sagging in all her body, a lassitude that made her waist look lopsided.

She understood, the day after her marriage,

the jealous hatred that divided those two, and a compensatory thought, a delicacy that her husband couldn't understand, made her adopt a humility, a grovelling dog-like docility as a kind of palliative for her mother's aggressive humor.

Pajadou saw immediately all the advantages he could draw from that submission, finally he succeeded in setting himself straight on his wife's intimate feelings after a violent scene wherein, in a fit of rage, the only time he could be reproached, he had come "this close" to killing a worker.

Héloïse was shocked, less by the new aspect in which Pajadou appeared to her, than by the scandal that a similar scene could have engendered. She loathed anything that drew attention to them, anything that, in their life together, lent an opportunity for comment. She feared, above all, the tittle-tattle and gossip that undresses a woman, betrays her secrets in the home, and passes comment on her sex life in the bedroom. She made the effacement of her life accord with the effacement of her person, and she dreamed of an intimateness behind closed doors, a corner where nothing from the outside could enter.

Pajadou, when he held all the important strings in his hand, was the master of the laundry. He worked less, without any concern for the two women yoked to a tough task and slogging away without respite. Finally, when the business expanded, he went to Paris two times a week by coach, Mondays and Fridays.

III

One day, when she had to do some shopping in Paris, Mother Vaillant found herself, on the tramway, beside Madame Ledieu, an old client who often held Héloïse on her knees when, still a child, she accompanied her father on his Monday rounds.

Without notice, Madame Ledieu had stopped doing business with the laundry. She gave vague reasons to explain her decision, according to Pajadou who, one evening, on returning home, had brought the news. It was a loss. Madame Ledieu, a pretty, little old lady, very pious, was the patroness of all the charities in her arrondissement. It was through her that Mother Vaillant had gotten a foot in the door at the sacristies and had gained the business at two boarding schools for young girls, not to mention a retirement home for old men.

The good woman's defection brought with it the business with the curates and the boarding schools. Mother Vaillant, vexed by this, did not appear disposed to hold a conversation with her former client, but Madame Ledieu went to sit beside her to inquire graciously about everyone's health. She had a pretty, caressing, and musical voice that you could say would have made you confess your innermost thoughts.

Mother Vaillant, who was politely reserved at first, gave in finally, and seemed to show interest in the saintly lady's stories. She was still very busy with visits to the poor, to the sick, to wet nurses; yes, to wet nurses! The Society for the Protection of New-

Born Children had solicited her help. Which meant that it was one problem after the next. She had just bought, with her very own money, little bonnets for the dear nannies' little cuties. And she showed her all the lingerie, the undershirts, the bibs, the wonderful bonnets that she held on her clenched hand. All of which induced Mother Vaillant to bring up the topic of their ruptured relationship.

Ah, yes! and why didn't she entrust her with her linen anymore?

Madame Ledieu feigned a great surprise.

"How's that! your son-in-law, he didn't tell you?..."

"Uh, well, yes, the poor people you wanted to help earn some money, but that wasn't the real reason..."

"Yes, really."

"Did we do something wrong? We never returned your linen in bad condition; we turned the work around quickly."

"No, no..."

Madame Ledieu, serious now, lowered her eyes, folded her baby clothes slowly.

"Are you certain there isn't something you're not telling me," responded the laundress, obstinately.

Madame Ledieu rose; this was her stop. And Mother Vaillant followed her, understanding that the little old woman didn't wish to speak about it on the tramway.

On the sidewalk, after two minutes of silence, Madame Ledieu, having collected herself, began:

"Well! I will tell you then..."

Whereupon, calmly, choosing her words carefully, without embarrassment however, she recounted that, when she returned home one Monday, unexpectedly, right at noon, she found Pajadou in bed with the maid.

"In my room, in my bed! You understand! I sent the girl packing, and I told your son-in-law that, from then on, I would do without his services. There, between you and me, could I have done any differently?"

Mother Vaillant turned completely white, then scarlet one instant later. She was suffocating, unable to find anything to say.

Moreover, Madame Ledieu, the incident noted, drew a thousand consequences from it.

"You have to understand," she said, "that our relationship had become impossible. Oh! I regret it terribly; I am sorry for you, you and Héloïse... But my duty, and prudence, advised me to protect the young girls at the boarding school... Oh! in other words! Goodness gracious! it could have happened there, a scene similar to what I had stumbled on. You see the scandal, yes! Hey! Your son-in-law, it appears, does that sort of thing regularly... Oh! I'm not asserting anything. I was told that a female cook... but those are just rumors! All the same, it must be quite annoying to you!"

And her pretty voice was a caress that strove to soften the bitterness of her revelations. She used her voice marvelously, attenuating the effrontery of certain words with the notes of a flute that affected the soul.

Madame Ledieu stopped, rue Denfert-Rochereau, at the door to a convent. But before entering, she concluded.

"You're upset with me, I know. Oh! it's very, very unfortunate! Everyone carries his own cross in this world!... We all have our Calvary that we climb."

She had tears in her voice, which she moistened with a contained sensibility, and a pretty little pout on her face. Then, all of a sudden, changing tone, she said:

"Most importantly, don't get my name mixed up in any of this business. I don't want to talk about it. I hate gossip!"

She modulated a "Goodbye, my dear lady!" in high notes and passed, smiling and precious, before the porter who doffed his cap upon seeing her.

IV

When Mother Vaillant returned home, after her shopping, a thousand ideas got muddled up in her head, leaving her undecided on how to proceed.

She had caught her son-in-law! That was her dominant thought, the victory cry that buzzed in her ears. She forgot about the injury done to her daughter, the prejudice that might result against her business as a result of the patron's debauchery, and all the griefs she was amassing converged on the same goal: to prove Pajadou guilty of interference, to relegate him to a subordinate position, to regain finally that authority that had escaped her.

Only, should she let Héloïse in on the secret of her husband's love affairs?

She was a good woman fundamentally and adored her daughter, but in a particular fashion.

She had a thorny exterior, a surly attitude; she liked how she talked, how she walked, – harshly. She let out sounds like certain women make love. Little things, childish details assumed an extraordinary importance by the exuberant life she attributed to them. The least of her movements betrayed a need to expend the intense energies of a plethoric woman.

It wasn't only her silences that became deafening but the way she moved her arms, turned her head, sat down.

She would have given both eyes in her head to make Héloïse happy, and her blood boiled to see her so calm with her white face, her measured gestures, her gentle tranquility. At that moment, Mother Vaillant said willfully that "she was every bit her father! – molten wax: no character!"

She recognized also that Héloïse took after her

mother in a dogged attachment to work, inflexible honesty, and above all the desire to keep the business – her father's business, – standing and intact!

Héloïse was ironing the linen, on the ground floor, when Mother Vaillant returned. She let herself fall back onto a chair with a kind of groaning sound, and what followed was silence, but one of those menacing silences that Mother Vaillant alone knew how to manage.

The flat headbands in ironer's hair glistened, and through an opening in her camisole a piece of her moist flesh could seen palpitating. From one moment to the next, she brought the iron close to her cheek. But her mother's attitude made her nervous; she asked: "What is it?"

"Just that," replied Mother Vaillant, "women are silly gooses with the temperament to work themselves to death while the male goes cock-a-doodle-doing about town!"

Héloïse, blinking her eyes, did not understand.

The other continued: – "That's what happens, when one stays locked up inside like this for weeks, one does not know... If only you knew!..."

Héloïse interrupted her work this time.

She put down the iron, and, looking at her mother, without commotion, she sighed: "If I told you that I know?"

But, standing on her feet, hands on her hips, her neck outstretched, the laundress had her doubts.

"You know he cheats on you?" she cried, betraying herself without thinking.

Héloïse responded, her voice lowered all of a sudden.

"Yes," she had surprised them embracing behind a door.

"Surprised!... who?..." In her turn, Mother Vaillant was mixing up the two stories, the one she knew and the one she was anticipating.

Héloïse had picked up her iron again, her eyes fixed on the ironing board:

"I've had my suspicions for a long time now, since my peritonitis, which confined me to bed for two months. When I was able to rise, I noticed that he was always caught up in the underskirts of the big redhead, that shameless hussy... it was bound to happen!"

Mother Vaillant was outraged by the calm with which her daughter recounted those things.

She groaned: "So, it's big red, huh? Ah! well, just a minute!..."

But as Mother Vaillant was reaching the door, with her enormous, rolling breasts, furiously shaking in her corsage, Héloïse stopped her with a blinking of the eyes.

"No scene, I beg you," she murmured; "tomorrow all the town will know that Pajadou sleeps with his workers."

Suddenly, the fat woman exploded. Her anger grew from a vexation: how is it she hadn't, prying woman that she was, discovered that liaison going on behind her back, under her roof?

She got it off her chest, cried: "Scoundrel! Scoundrel! Scoundrel!" They had told her, in any case, what that Pajadou was like: a whoremonger, a skirt chaser, nothing more! Ah! She knew that her marriage to him would not change anything; it was in his blood!

Héloïse protested, pleading seduction, a continual provocation by the girl...

Then Mother Vaillant forgot herself, got the two stories mixed up in her head, got all worked up by the contradiction.

"Well, yes," she said, "I'll give you that. And the others? Madame Ledieu's maid, and the cook, and all the other sluts one does not know about! I suppose they too seduced him, huh?"

Héloïse repeated her words automatically: "Madame Ledieu... the cook..." without understanding, but guessing vaguely. Her mother had caught her off guard. She walked forward, then back, stewed in her juices, pounding her fist on the table with hissing exclamations: "That's beautiful. And you forgive him!"

"I haven't told you in fact..."

Then she told for her, in a trembling, but lowered voice, the scene she heard about from Madame

Ledieu. But a moment later a furious rage seized her again. She cried out:

"You know what? Well, he's gonna ruin us, we'll be out on the street I tell you!"

Héloïse felt faint. Bars, like those that, on images, represent lightening, zigzagged before her eyes, and she had to lean against the wall so as not to fall.

The two women grew silent, a sudden moment of peace lulled them into a kind of blessed cowardice, a weakening discouragement.

Héloïse sat down again. In this way, that domestic shame she was familiar with, that she could reach out and touch with her hand, and that she had, for modesty's sake, kept hidden deep within herself, triply locked up, – that filth was escaping, leaking out, running though the streets! She went over the offense in her mind, went straight to the scandal and to its probable consequences: a defection of clients bringing the laundry to its ruin. She was not a bourgeois, a pretentious woman lamenting over her husband's infidelity, looking for traps and interventions in order to catch her husband in the arms of another woman! What did she ask of her husband, now that the sum total of faithfulness that she could expect from him was known? Was it launched from his loves at the laundry? Had she reproached him for those? No; she had hoped that by closing her eyes to his affairs with the workers, she could deflect him from chasing skirts in public, villainous and compromising as that might have been. And now we have clients finding him in their bed with their maids!

Mother Vaillant asked suddenly: "Do you want me to speak to him?"

"No", Héloïse responded; "tomorrow, we will see."

"Tomorrow! You really are your father's daughter! That's some will for you!"

Héloïse made a supplicating gesture that signified: "Ah! why are you all badgering me!..."

Totally shaken, she found it hard to breathe, and her eyes were blinded. She didn't notice her mother had left the room, but suddenly she heard an argument break out on the floor above. The word: "slut! slut!" which Mother Vaillant hurled at the top of her lungs, could be heard above the others.

Héloïse, leaving her work, went to the stairwell, where she could hear the phrases more clearly. Pajadou and his mother-in-law were yelling at each other furiously. The laundress had slapped big red's face, screaming at her never to set foot in the house again, and Pajadou wouldn't have any of it, nobody could chase his workers off without consulting with him first. Who was the boss? Him or her? He gave in finally however; he took the position of leaving in order to avoid a scene, but the mother-in-law stopped him in his tracks with one phrase: "Ah, yes! That's good, go find your redhead whore!"

She hurled that phrase at his back, in a total rage. Pajadou turned about; he hesitated, then, seeing himself alone with her, he was seized with a anger; with a piercing voice, he let her have it. Yes, he had slept with the redhead. And then? She wasn't the first, or the last, and anyone who didn't like it could come and tell him about it to his face!...

"I think Madame Ledieu has already seen to that," replied Mother Vaillant.

He had a small start, then responded, contemptibly:

"Madame Ledieu? That Goody Two-Shoes! That presbyter's bedbug!"

After those two strong phrases, the laundress thought she'd take a different tack, work on his feelings a bit.

"You ought to be ashamed of yourself," she said, growing calm now, "ashamed to lead a life like that in front of your children and your wife!"

His wife! The word exasperated him. "So she's the one who sent you, huh?"

He squinted maliciously, happy to take out on the daughter the forward thrusts of the mother. "Tell Héloïse I'll find outside what I don't find at home! I still got a bit of life in me... I'm not made o' wood like your daughta, you know? We sleep in the same bed just for show; she acts like an old woman."

He left the room. The laundress shouted after him: "Jesuit!" but as she was getting ready to pursue him, she saw Héloïse who, hidden at the end of the hallway, hadn't missed a word of their conversation. The two women saw all their anguish, all their despair, in each other's glance. Mother Vaillant felt a sudden pang of motherly tenderness, one of those rare moments of breakdown, which brought a flood of tears to her eyes, which fell onto her chest brusquely, accompanied by loud sobs! It was just another way of expending her pent up anger and frustration in life.

For an hour, an old affection for the child hiding behind the badly-married and teary-eyed woman, jostled her amassed rancors, penetrated her all the same. She took Héloïse into her arms; and she kissed her hair, cried into her neck. Suddenly she covered her with her body, trying to protect her from hearing Pajadou who was whistling a tune in the courtyard.

V

From the time of that scene, life at the laundry was, for the two women, a disquietude; they were on their guard at every instant. Mother Vaillant, as if to punish herself for not having, from the beginning, uncovered her son-in-law's tricks, organized a system of spying, a continuous harassment. She followed him around with furious eyes, a machine's wheezing, and the swish of her skirts in the sweep of a broom. He found her everywhere, in the attic, in the cellar, in the drying room, in the workshop, and that silent shadowing exasperated him like a threat of danger by which an enemy retards the effect in order to prolong the pleasure of exacting vengeance. She never attacked Pajadou directly, but she slapped the girls who left him, still warm and flushed from his arms!

Then there were the muted battles, the pulling

of hair, the scratching of nails, and the terrible biting!

The girl remained at the laundry long enough for the boss had draw all the sensual delights from her charms that he had promised himself.

Pajadou had dropped his mask around the family, but outside the home, or in front of strangers at the laundry, the man transformed himself with a feline suppleness. He was a good boy with heavy eyelids, swollen face, half-asleep, an inoffensive person measuring his words, caressing his children, greeting his wife with a kind word.

Héloïse, with a profound penetration, a secret knowledge of her husband, a silent and shrouded observation, was the only person who could say, just by looking at Pajadou, which woman he coveted. In front of this woman, he curled up into a ball, with the half-closed eyes of a lascivious cat, an atony in his face, the game people play with their eyelids when they are blinded by sunlight. And he licked his lips with little swipes of the tongue, folded over on himself, pickled in a quietude that enlarged his cheeks.

Héloïse, with an air of resigned detachment, suffered a thousand deaths. This thirty-two-year-old woman had the body of a duenna, wrinkled from feet to face. When she suspended, at rare moments of repose, the bestial labor that deadened her grief, to lull her troubles to sleep, it was to inquire into the critical remarks that she believed her family was the object of in town.

She fell ill for two days on learning that a

worker, Pajadou's mistress, had recounted the story of her love affair, a little bit everywhere, in order to get back at her ex-lover for having dumped her.

That snippet of gossip that corroborated certain stories, which malicious tongues had spread, caused a scandal in the community.

How's that! Monsieur Pajadou!

It was now "Monsieur Pajadou," the owner.

The boss of the laundry had knocked off the skirt chaser, the lone, irresistible bachelor-knight of ancient festive balls. Then he returned to the wine merchant's place, which he had abandoned since his marriage for the most part. He called out to passersby at the hour of absinthe, offering them a round. Adroitly he maneuvered the conversation to the topic of women, and, seated at a corner of the table, with wily innuendos, he got around to talking about the affair himself, with the girl who had blabbed. My God, yes; it wasn't a secret! Hold on! That wasn't all there was to say about it, – fortunately! Besides, there was the blood; the blood had always annoyed him!

Nobody could really hold it against a man who acted in that way, who confessed his little affairs on the side. And people laughed even when he insinuated that his wife, – oh! a good and honest woman! – always ill, weak-blooded, shirked her marriage duties, which his strong male appetite demanded strict adherence to.

He said these things calmly, threw out a crude word to paint a picture and help in the understanding of his confidences. And the laughers being on his side, he easily won the case. All the women were for him. They detested Héloïse and her mother, the old hags who never rubbed elbows with anyone and always kept at a distance. One laundress, tall and flat, made this remark even: that quite a few women would have considered themselves lucky to have married such a man!

So Pajadou, with the strong support he found outside the home as payment for his audacity, had all the workers on his side. He had two mistresses at the same time, interfering with the work in order to play. He hired a second fellow and stopped working altogether, limiting his responsibilities to surveillance only, which authorized his idleness, whispering, and the petting behind closed doors.

In Paris, which he visited two times a week, he brought along a boy who watched the wagon while he called on clients. Héloïse interrogated the kid. She learned that Pajadou often stayed one hour at a house on rue Grétry, across the street from the Opéra-Comique. She consulted the books. The only clients they had on that street were the Josèphe ladies, three single women without a profession apparently. Héloïse didn't see the need to question the child any further, but one evening at dinnertime, she hazarded this observation:

"Do you know that the Josèphes owe us 80 francs?"

Pajadou, called out, responded:

"Ah!... There's no hurry! They'll pay, for goodness' sake!"

Héloïse didn't insist; she simply asked her mother, the following day, who those ladies were. The good woman didn't know; clients brought in by Pajadou, clearly.

Now, life for Héloïse was becoming intolerable between her husband and her mother. She especially dreaded the meal hour when the family got together around the table. Everyone ate in silence, seriously. But Mother Vaillant had so expressive a mobility in the look on her face, she found such tones of voice to use when asking for the bread, accompanied by darting eyes filled with daggers, that Héloïse often lost her appetite, pushed her plate aside, stared up at the ceiling, dreaming. Or she would say to her mother: "Please, change your expression, you take my appetite away!"

Then the large woman got up from the table, her mouth twisted! "Fine! Seeing as I'm bothering you!" She carried her meal with her into the kitchen and finished eating at a corner of the table. But a continuous buzzing, an obsessive grumbling by the stubborn old woman, pierced through the wall like the refrain that an organ grinds out and that sticks in your head for a long time afterwards.

VI

Pajadou for a long time now treated himself to whole days off. In addition to the trips he was forced to

make on Mondays and Fridays, he went to Paris at the
drop of a hat, without notice, in the afternoon. Léontine, who was his mistress at the laundry at that time,
was surprised that their love affair, barely started, had
been interrupted like that. Héloïse, very disquieted,
sensed a new blow. Mother Vaillant, going on vague
indications, had made two trips to Paris, without re-
sults. Finally, she used some subterfuge to introduce
herself naturally at the Josèphe ladies' house. She de-
livered in person to them a camisole that she had by
design removed from the packet of linen Pajadou
brought back with him. She was received by an old
woman with gray corkscrew curls in her hair and
wearing a peignoir with a leafy design on it. Another
woman, younger, also in peignoir, but all white, with
very short sleeves, half-opened a door, popped her
head of tousled hair out, and disappeared again shout-
ing: "Not to worry, it's nobody!"

Mother Vaillant, quite well received otherwise, noticed however, in the one room that she was
received in, the framed image of an enormous swan,
its beak voluptuously placed between the two naked
breasts of a sprawling woman. But back on the street,
lifting her eyes, the laundress noticed a young woman
in the window, her third client apparently, who was
sewing. She wore, like a flag, one of those long
camisoles, called matinées, and cast out onto the
street, frequently, long glances that took in all the
length of the rue de Marivaux, as far as the corner of
the Opéra-Comique.

One evening, on his return home, Pajadou
went straight to bed and told someone to go fetch the

doctor. The two women were not admitted to the con-
sultation given by the doctor to the launderer. Pajadou
kept to his bed for two months. A ring of spots dotted
his face; his hair fell out. They came to see him and
pitied him all the more since he moaned with every
movement that he made, attributing his illness to the
effort he had made unloading the packets of linen.
The doctor said his illness was a... a hernia... Ah! No
medication, no drugs, no bandages, nothing!

Also, the tables in his room were not encum-
bered with vials or pharmaceutical products, – in
front of visitors at least. But Pajadou who, in reality,
followed a strict regimen, had prescriptions by the
doctor prepared for him in Paris and followed them to
the letter, but behind closed doors, without anyone
being the wiser.

One detail stood out to Héloïse however. Her
husband, at the start of his illness, asked her point-
blank: "Have the Josèphes paid?"

"No, they haven't."

He flew into a rage, swore, treated them like
whores who should be thrown into prison... or some-
place else! But immediately he regretted that last bit,
and, to cover up for his equivocal appearance, he
added that "they couldn't afford to lose twenty-four
francs like that." Finally, one Monday, Mother Vaillant, who was doing the rounds for the son-in-law,
brought back those ladies' response: "Let Monsieur
Pajadou come in person; we will settle with him face
to face!" He didn't respond and didn't bring it up
again.

His anxiety at the beginning of his illness, dissipated by the doctor, was revived at certain moments. Then the words of a friend, who had shared the life of a bachelor with him, came back to his memory. "You," his friend said to him, patting him familiarly on the stomach, "a little lower, it's through that pipe there that you will empty yourself!"

At the end of the second month, he entered into full convalescence. He got up out of bed, stood standing in front of the window for most of the day, bored stiff. Cured finally, he could go about his business. And his hair grew back with a wave to it that he didn't have before his illness.

He seldom went out at first, put his life in order. To Léontine's advances, he gave a cold shoulder, which disconcerted her. Vexed, she was absent now for several days in a row. Héloïse found herself rejoicing over that illness, which seemed to have returned a corrected husband to her. Also, she didn't dare take advantage of the female worker's absences to dismiss her, for fear that a commotion might send the boss back into the girl's arms, attracting attention to her again.

She did right. One Saturday evening, Léontine came on her own initiative and did exactly as she had desired.

"I'm leaving; pay up!"

Héloïse, happy at heart, thought she should feign surprise.

"I'm leaving, I said! pay me," said the worker.

She left without saying goodbye, without going to look for Pajadou. She met up with, that same evening, on the route to Orléans, a man wearing a top hat who was waiting for her.

Then, side by side, they disappeared into the night.

VII

Héloïse had several good months. Pajadou seemed to have taken a vow of continence, and Mother Vaillant relaxed her guard-dog-like surveillance that was no longer warranted.

Héloïse didn't demand that her husband return to work immediately; it could be, she thought, that rubbing elbows daily with the female workers would cause his flesh and his blood to be whipped up again in all senses of the phrase. Pajadou then could give himself over to the calm of what he called a restorative repose. He acquired a habit of idleness and egotistical well-being perfectly in line with his temperament and previously devised plans.

Héloïse, after a rough day at work, liked to come and sit in the courtyard, which formed a long square separating the main house, with its facade to the street, and the workshops built opposite it. Her happy childhood was spent there. She attached a memory to each of the three floors, on the ground floor where the linen was sorted out and where the workers ironed it; then, one floor up, in the rooms they inhabited; finally, in the loft, which served as a vast dryer that she adored and that was really the physiognomy of the house with its windows without glass, its large beams from which thin cords hung and ran, and its perches stretching their skinny, skeleton-like arms into the void, between the open windows.

She relived her schooldays, still hearing the good sister reciting the "*Je vous salue, Marie....*" She returned to the laundry area, cast a glance at the hangar, at the poles supporting the crosspieces where the linen would be stretched out, and ran into the workshop, which attracted her with its two vast vats, the reservoir, and the washing tub that the horse turned. Then she ran back to the courtyard, with its rabbit hutches, and she engaged in interminable con-versations with them, while curling their fine whiskers, or with the dog, or with the horse, interpret-ing their silent astonishment, devising both questions and answers. Sometimes she disputed with the hens, which pecked at the dirty weeds in the courtyard, a slice of bread with moldy jam that she end up aban-doning to them, her hands scratched.

Those were happy hours! She grew up in the sun, in the smell of detergent, and in the acrid per-fume of warm steam that fermenting manure filled the air with, beside the truck farmlands.

Her mother was always the same woman, be-hind whom, intimidated by her corpulence, and the truly imposing breadth of her backside, Monsieur Vaillant, her father, was effaced, and disappeared, with his narrow, short, and spineless body, with his low forehead, and his nose like a knife blade.

Héloïse still had before her eyes an image of the poor man's trepidations, his humble demeanor of a beaten dog, living in the shadow of its master. Never a revolt! He bent over, under his wife, just as he did under the bundles of linen that he carried, – by force of habit. It was that spiritually annulled man who declared, on his deathbed, while holding his wife's hands in his own, that the dear creature had made him very happy!

The laundry remained in the hands of the two women. Héloïse lived the day all over again when she first noticed Pajadou among the workers; they exchanged a glance, and she vaguely felt that that glance bound them, riveted them together, forever. They hadn't even exchanged a word until fifteen days later; they even avoided running into each other. Only Pajadou, in order to belie the insinuations of people who made him out to be a skirt chaser, someone who spent all his leisure time outside the laundry partying and in attempts at picking up girls, affected the peaceful demeanor of an orderly fellow. He spent all his evenings on the street, a cigarette in mouth, with an absorbed air.

And behind a window on the second floor, a shadow passed, that disappeared when Pajadou was out of sight. Then, one day, without premeditation, they found themselves face to face and alone. He took her in his arms and pressed her against his breast for a long time without saying a word.

Anyone other than Héloïse would "have gotten it," to employ Pajadou's expression; but he respected her, out of self-interest, wanting to take her not when she gave herself to him, but when she was given to him.

She was given to him. Héloïse, now that she recalled the scene she had had with her mother, was surprised to have shown that firmness, that energy that she didn't think she was capable of today. Mother Vaillant, it is true, consented to the marriage only by having had her hand forced, she said. Having gathered information on him, she couldn't get around Pajadou's thirty-five years of debauched living which she would have forgiven in an inexperienced and curious young man.

One had even, charitably, pointed out to Héloïse several liaisons that Pajadou had had with some women of Arcueil, but the young girl had received those confidences and those warnings with the proper contempt of a woman who knows herself presently to be loved. Her natural uprightness made it a duty with her not to be jealous of her husband's past, a dead flame that he would bury under the lukewarm ashes of marriage without ever thinking to stoke them again.

The first years of married life had been happy with the four births that, in spite of their fatiguing succession, were still causes for joy. Héloïse hadn't noticed that maternity had withered her, faded her complexion. Work at the laundry, made more difficult each day by expansion of the business, and the needs of the children whom she had to feed, left her no time to spend in front of the mirror in order to find a way to attenuate the crow's feet, the precocious lines on her nose, the tan of her cheeks.

Internally, her soul alone received the impressions, felt the pricks and strains, but the envelope remained impenetrable, the mask bore no frown; beneath the mask however the flesh bled, cried, felt shattered. The mute hostility that reigned between her husband and her mother had not bothered her much. She thought that time would get the better of that base rancor and would reunite those two enemies, those two forces who would work together for the greater glory of the laundry. For Héloïse felt certain that she was, between those two, the arm that works, not the head that thinks, not the initiative that decides. The blood of her father flowing through her veins had had too great an influence on her organization, so that she could remove herself from that continual hesitation, leading her to accept everything that happened without a fight or at least without an effective defense. Also, she worked non-stop, like a beast of burden, and those contrasts were surprising for the observer: her physical body accepted valiantly life's constant battle and put on a good outward show in the melee, but her moral system was spineless, impotent, null; that extreme sensibility of heart and that abandonment of her intellectual "me" were the result.

After his first offense, – Pajadou's carnal appetencies would inevitably gain the upper hand, – Héloïse began to climb her Calvary. The cut was deep, but the hemorrhage was internal. She wore, for those near her, a mask to hide her grief, in order to prevent scandal and gossip from gaining ground. She didn't put up a fight, understanding that she had lost in advance that unequal battle between her malleable femininity and Pajadou's experienced wiliness.

And these were the things Héloïse was thinking about, in the evening, in the courtyard of the laundry. Now that Pajadou seemed corrected, she began to experience hope again. Age assisting, with the flesh calmed, he toed the line and acted the part of husband and father.

A canary, in a cage hung on the wall, launched its piercing "tweet!... tweet!... tweet!..." crowned by roulades and trills; a breeze stirred the scrawny plants along the edges, behind a row of laid bricks, and a tubercular vine climbed amongst the large-headed nails and iron wires twisted under the zinc conduits.

VIII

"M'sieu Pajadou!... Hey, boss!"

Pajadou turned round and saw Carniche who, from his doorsill, called out to him. The launderer walked back.

Carniche was a day laborer in Gentilly. He lived there with his wife and daughter on the ground floor, in an apartment with two small, very clean rooms. The first was where the family worked; in the evening, they set up a bed there for the little one. In the second room slept the parents.

Carniche was a character, the hard-working type, tough, stubborn, avid for gain, but of a strict honesty. He gave himself, each day, no more than half an hour of rest, not including mealtimes. He worked for the truck farmers, all week long; on Sundays, he worked for the bourgeois, turning the soil in their gardens, and at other small jobs. Finally, at home, in the evening, he made packing cases for a confectioner, or fishing nets. He forbade himself any pastime that was harmful to his interests, – reading the newspaper, hanging out in bars, – and he didn't allow his wife or his daughter to stand in front of him with their arms dangling. Madame Carniche was a little, peaky creature, humble, unassuming, who did housework, assisted the sick, babysat and helped her husband in the fabrication of nets. She had a resigned-looking face, calmly sad, where her very gentle eyes, like two blue flowers, shone. But with her toothless mouth, she appeared older than her husband, although she was barely thirty-six years old.

"What may I do for you, father Carniche?" said Pajadou entering.

At that moment, while his wife was lighting the lamp, Carniche spoke his business. He had decided that his little one would no longer go back to school; having sent her there until she was thirteen years old, he believed he had done his duty. In brief, he wanted to find a job for the girl, somewhere she could be useful and learn a trade.

"With you, for example, Monsieur Pajadou, as an apprentice..."

Having come straight out with the request, Carniche, figuring he had just wasted ten minutes of his time, picked up a handful of nails that he put into his mouth, then, with hammer in hand, striking softly enough so that it would not drown out his voice, he continued talking, while he worked his way around a case: "You see, M'sieu Pajadou, it's time that everyone at home worked: the little one as well as the mother! I work hard, me! You don't think we can have her sitting around doing nothing; she's not a bourgeoise. So she will learn before too long how to serve her bosses honestly and earn a living. I've already given one year's credit to her mother, who thinks Reine to be delicate, immature...

"It's nonsense! Work will mature her; she needs to work!"

But he noticed Madame Carniche in front of him, tears welling in her eyes...

"You got nothing to do, woman?"

She quickly lowered her head, without recrimination, and moved her agile fingers, which were trembling a little. The door opened. Reine entered. She said "bonjour" without any embarrassment to Pajadou whom she recognized.

"I was thinking," said Carniche to the launderer, "I thought... well, what do you say?"

"You understand," Pajadou responded, "I need to speak with Héloïse first, but I think she'll consent to have your child as an apprentice." He turned to face Reine:

"Would you be happy working for us?"

She murmured, "Yes, Monsieur."

"Well, alright then, I'll take care of this; send her tomorrow morning to the laundry."

Pajadou departed, his arms crossed behind his back, walking slowly.

Carniche went back to his case again; he looked at Reine planted before him thinking, and growled: "Come here! Take this! You will glue the paper onto the box... that will always be more useful than watching flies sleep!"

IX

The following morning, Madame Carniche accompanied Reine to the laundry. Pajadou was absent, they were received by Héloïse, who had been brought up-to-speed by her husband.

Reine was not yet fourteen years old; she looked twelve, if that. She was small in stature, very slender, with an immensely sweet prettiness. Her very blond and very fine hair were tucked up under a little white bonnet pulled down over her ears. But what was particularly pretty about her was her complexion. Her white skin, a transparent, delicately pink white skin, which her eyelashes cast a shadow on, gave her a luminous face: it was like a spray of flowers held together in the hands of a child who would have forgotten on purpose, in order to adorn her looks, the bluets of her eyes and the coquelicots on her lips, in the mad shoots of blond curls that escaped from under her bonnet.

Such as she was, with her scrawny chicken legs, her arms like batten, and her formless body of a child who grew in height, she immediately pleased Héloïse. On the following day, she entered into their service. She came from Gentilly in the morning, by traversing Arcueil. Her father accompanied her and came back for her in the evening; but it was a rather large waste of his time, so that he renounced stopping to visit with Pajadou when they arrived, and he turned around immediately for Gentilly. The little girl went alone then, subsequently, but sometimes a female worker from Arcueil walked back with her.

One evening, Léontine presented herself at the laundry, saying that she wanted to see the patroness. Reine went to find her and left the two women alone, under the hangar.

Léontine had quit her job two months earlier; Héloïse thought she had come to ask for her job back, but she was quickly disabused: Léontine laid down the facts, proudly. She was pregnant. The child's father was not faraway; this particularity, she thought, would make Héloïse do something for her... She wasn't demanding. She was simply in need of a place to give birth tranquilly, in a hotel bed, it didn't matter where; that's all she was asking for. If not, hell! The first step at the front door would serve as a pillow!

Héloïse, taken aback, protested nonetheless:

"Come on! My husband..."

Then the girl, who had not explained herself categorically, clearly asserted that Pajadou was the fa-

ther. "One could question him. I would love to see
him try and deny it!" She added:

"What's done is done! Only, I cannot give
birth like a dog, on the street, can I? I haven't worked
for over three days now and I haven't got cent to my
name. If I don't pay in advance, for a hotel room, they
will throw me out. Ah! I have no other choice than to
come here and ask you for a bed!"

Héloïse was disconcerted, she imagined the
girl setting herself up there, and she knew she was capable of dragging her child all around the countryside
proclaiming the parentage that united it to Pajadou.

Léontine waited for an answer, sure of herself, with all the aplomb of a crafty bitch. She was the
cat that brings the mouse back coldly; she hadn't
made any effort to see the boss; but if Héloïse wanted
to call him, go ahead!

The girl certainly wasn't lying. She had an
enormous belly, and her face looked ravaged, with
traits drawn, and skin yellow.

"How much do you need!" asked Héloïse.

Léontine responded: "I'd need fifty francs."

"A little brat is expensive! Isn't that right!
And then a natural person can't just go giving birth
like an animal!"

Héloïse told her to hold on. She disappeared
and came back a moment later with a banknote which
she gave to the girl; but when she turned on her heels
without saying goodbye, without so much as a thank

you, the laundress called her back and, without doubting that she would comply, made her swear to keep it a secret.

"Come on! That's stupid!" sniggered the worker.

On leaving, she crossed Pajadou and pretended not to see him. She rejoined, in the avenue de Cachau, a man, her lover, who was waiting for her. This man was named Pavanne, a hale and hearty man of thirty-five years, ugly, with a pockmarked face, a toothbrush mustache, a pug nose, glassy eyes, hair balding in the front and combed forward toward the temples, straight and shiny. He looked like a street pedlar, a crafty fellow, a hooligan, agile like a clown, wily like a policeman, with a laugh like a monkey, showing its rotten teeth, his patter like a street performer's, a dexterity that he hid as well as his infernal volubility beneath a feigned nonchalance, a nasal and drawling voice, with a gallivanter's abandon.

He said he knew all the professions without having practiced one of them. Léontine was solidly attached to him from the moment she saw him working at the festival in Neuilly. Three-card trick player emeritus, he had her in the palm of his hand, while emptying her pockets gently at first, then fleecing the silly goose that she was whom the player's imperturbable aplomb, his ferocious trick, held under his spell.

He showed himself, that day, as generous. After having robbed the girl, as she stood planted in front of him, with silent admiration in her eyes, he offered her some swill and a bed. Now it was she who was supporting him, him being flat broke. So delicate for all that! He didn't ask her to provide for them from the product of her good fortune walking the streets, an honest and lucrative employment was more suitable for her. Thus, he got the benefit of her employment, not the burdens!

They left together, the two of them, down to the gate.

"Did she fork it over?" asked Pavanne.

She responded: "Yep."

"Fifty?"

"Fifty."

She saw his hand held out, and she slipped the banknote into it.

"Nice! He owes you that much, the dirty bastard!"

"The father!... the father!..." she repeated, as if she had a doubt suddenly in her mind; and she looked at him with her amorous, very expressive eyes.

But he warded her off: "You're crazy! Just say it was him... They'll fork it over!"

She asked: "You're going to the festival at Nogent, Monday?"

"Maybe."

So she promised to go and see him at work. It

was a whim that she often had. The suckers' alarm, the way he fleeced them, delighted her, gave her a gallant idea of her man.

Pajadou, who had seen Léontine leaving the laundry, asked Héloïse what she had come for.

"She has no place to go," said Héloïse; "she asks for her job back."

"You said no, I hope?"

"I said no."

That "I hope," offhand like that, seemed to her like the condemnation of a bad past, the promise of a better future. She felt a warm feeling that descended on her and penetrated her with a great feeling of well-being. That one phrase had the efficacy of a balm to close the cut that the lunatic woman had just re-opened. Then again, wasn't that already an ancient wound? And, completely set at ease again, Héloïse said that she had just paid fifty francs to bury it, to put an end forever to a past that one didn't wish to hear spoken of again.

The following day, which was Friday, Madame Carniche came, unannounced, to check in on her daughter at the laundry.

"Well, Madame Pajadou, are you satisfied with my little one? She's not yet too strong at the present moment..."

Timidly, she insinuated that the heavy load would crush her, ruin her health, – and, suddenly, afraid she had gone too far, she added that she was

quite at ease otherwise and that Reine could not have
found better employers.

Héloïse had taken a liking to the child. She
was amused by her calm candor, her eyes with their
chaste effrontery.

"Reine is full of good will," she said.

The wagon had just entered the courtyard.

Pajadou was furious. "You know, Héloïse," he
shouted, "this is the last time I am bringing the little
Gervais girl with me. The fact of the matter is that
this toad, instead of watching the wagon while I went
to speak with the clients, amused herself by playing
on the sidewalk with hooligans! I've informed her father!"

"That's annoying," said Héloïse; "who will
you have accompany you?"

"Bah! we have time to think about that. If I
can't find anyone else, Reine will come with me.
Would you like that, little one?"

She jumped for joy and said: "Yes," with
grateful eyes.

Pajadou, for form's sake, consulted Madame
Carniche: "Do you have any objection, mother?"

She responded that, on the contrary, she was
quite happy with that plan which assured Reine would
have two days a week of quasi repose.

"It's agreed then," concluded Pajadou; "only I
have to warn you that, in the event Reine makes the

rounds with me, she will be forced to spend the night here Monday. We come back too late for her to be able to go home alone."

Mother Carniche approved, gave her husband's consent, and took the girl home with her, who was delighted by the idea of those promenades in a wagon.

She was already asking herself what name she would give to the horse.

X

Mondays and Fridays were the days the little Carniche girl liked best. She had, on her first outings, a thousand surprises, a thousand little joys as a result of her imperfect knowledge of Paris, where her mother had conducted her rarely.

It was summer: the departure, the stop at the toll booth for the wagon's entry, then the confusion, the swarms of people, the animals and the things in the streets, the gaiety, the movement of the crowd, the little nothings that attract one's attention, for a moment; then, these kinds of banalities were an event: soldiers exiting the barracks, two carriages that collide, a dead horse waiting for the knacker in the midst of two hundred people, very attentive, standing up on their tiptoes to get a good look.

Reine had all the surprises of a Parisian street urchin, even though she was from the country. A grimacing monkey on a barrel organ left her wide-eyed

and charmed. She loved it when Pajadou went inside
to visit with the client. Then she took possession of
the wagon, spread her little dress out on the bench
and, her hands folded in her lap, sat upright and serious with the absorbed attitude of a grown up who
dreams of things.

They were hers, the wagon and the baskets
piled up in the back of it, hers the massive and tranquil horse. Sometimes, she got down, placed herself
at the head of the beast with the vague idea that she
made it respect her. But the hour of day she preferred
most was the hour of breakfast. Pajadou brought her
to a restaurant on rue Feydeau.

A restaurant! She had only heard about them,
and, when her secret desire to eat in one had been satisfied, she asked herself if she hadn't just, utterly
awake, dreamt what she had considered unrealizable!
They sat down close to the front door, in order to
watch the horse and wagon parked alongside the sidewalk. And Reine wrapped them in the same deference
– the restaurant customers, the office workers dressed
in black with their bored attitudes, and the boys she
thought she should thank with a silent admiration,
with long enraptured silences that took her appetite
away. She blushed, feeling ashamed, under the looks
of the gentlemen, or when the waiters asked her again
for the name of a plate of food she had asked for.

Pajadou was very good to her; he spoke to her
rarely and had a preoccupied air. She had a consider-
able respect for him, and she was always afraid to
lose, by being disagreeable to him, the benefit of
those fine trips on Mondays and Fridays.

Pajadou, he was the boss, the all-powerful man who could, with one word, send her back to her parents. And she found him very good, because he wanted to keep her on.

One Monday, they didn't return to the laundry before nine-thirty in the evening. After dinner, Héloïse released the little girl, for whom she had made up a bed, in a large room, where, in the winter, the wringers were operated. That was the moment Reine feared the most. She shuddered, alone at the end of the courtyard, above the workshop, in that vast room where, in the summer, some linen was stretched out to dry, when the attic and the driers were full. She went to bed, closed her eyes, wishing to fall asleep immediately. Then sleep being slow to come, she was taken by sudden fears. Her sleeplessness then, traversed by phantoms, terrified her. Women's long chemises seemed like hanging bodies swinging at the end of ropes; there were hanged men who detached themselves, walked towards her with a clattering of bones under the floating cloth... Cold things whisked past her; little by little, around her, everything took on an accentuated form: desperate and flabby arms rose from baskets, decapitated bodies walked about, danced an infernal dance in front of her bed. And handkerchiefs like enormous geometrids, wings spread, hovered for a moment and crashed into her frightened face... She let out a small cry, hid her head under the blanket, and end up by falling asleep finally, her body wet and shaken with shivers.

XI

"You like éclairs, I believe," said Pajadou.

The wagon stopped, he got down, entered a pastry shop and brought back an éclair for Reine, who was surprised. They resumed their journey. Pajadou, ordinarily a quiet man surprised the child. She had noticed, after lunch, that he had emptied the small carafe of brandy, which he usually only took a small glass of.

When they had passed the fortifications, he made the horses go at a walking pace. It was getting dark.

"Hell! Ten o'clock," said Pajadou, who had consulted his watch. "Anyone's guess if we will have time to get back before the storm."

Reine had wanted to tell him, because the horse was making them late, to whip it instead of slow it down; but Pajadou guessed what she was thinking.

"Too bad the horse is tired," he said.

To the day's blistering heat was added a harsh, blinding wind that collected the dust and blew it in dust devils with a sound of crumpled dried leaves. There were short periods of silence during which the horse's little bells tinkled, then a formidable gust swept the road clean, drove wisps of dust down the sidewalks... While passing in front of the fortifications, on the embankment and in the ditches, couples, lying on their stomach, lifted themselves, disquieted, and considered leaving. Now the shadows grew extended, the casement windows clacked; here and there, in the facade of dark houses, a luminous windowpane burst.

In the sky was a mad dash of thick clouds that pursued each other, bumped into each other, entered each other. Suddenly, on the horizon, other masses of clouds erected a high, dark wall across the road.

Reine and Pajadou chatted.

She recounted her mother's terrors when it thundered; she hid herself in the space between the bed and the wall...

"I knew before my marriage," said the launderer, "I knew a woman who collapsed and passed out during a storm, she even..."

He darted a glance at Reine and drowned the end of his phrase in a muffled laugh that seemed to turn away the memory of things that children ought not to know.

A silence ensued; girls passed by them running; one of them stopped and cried out:

"Ah! Blast it! My eyes are full of dust!"

She stood in the middle of the sidewalk, without a hat on; the wind trussed up her skirts and the white marks of her socks stood out in the shadows. The other girls had stopped, waited for her at a distance while bursting out with raffish laughter, the fits and starts of a gaggle of factory escapees.

Pajadou resumed: "Nasty weather! We won't be able to hang the linen out in the courtyard." Changing subjects suddenly, he added: "You know, looking at us, one would think we were husband and wife, don't you think, Reine?"

She lifted her eyes to look at him; his beard brushed her face and she lowered her head sharply, not realizing he was so near to her.

They didn't pass any other people along this stretch of the way. On their left, the open doors of some dives, poorly lit, leprous; but on the right, suddenly the line of houses was interrupted. They were in the fields now, the truck gardeners' plots that, on that side, bordered the road. The somber masses of manure looked like tumulary mounds in the shadows, and the handle of a pitchfork planted at the summit looked like a cross whose arms had been amputated. Then, the Montrouge Fort stood out in silhouette, but vaguely, as if crushed by the clouds, made smaller under the flattening of a low sky.

Now it was nothing but fields that bordered the road on both sides, left and right.

Two soldiers crossed it, in front of the wagon, and took a small path that led to the fort. They marched quickly, growing smaller in height the further they sank into the night; in the end, their broad backs were nothing more than two black points that disappeared around a bend in the path.

Reine let out a cry; she thought that a jolt of the wagon had just thrown her backwards. Her bonnet fell off and she felt a warm breath pass over her hair. Pajadou had let go of the reins... he was standing in front of her, his hands fumbling...

Reine could think that it was a swerve of the horse, and not a voluntary fall that threw him down beside her, in the back of the wagon, on the linen packets. And as she lost consciousness, her head seemed to her like an enormous bell where the little bells of the horse banged into each other and jingled and jangled continuously.

XII

Reine had, on awakening the following day, the vague and stupidly surprised look on her face of people who try to make some sense, in their mind, of memories from the day before and dreams during the night.

Little by little, however, her eyes opened, and the events of the memorable day unfolded, unwound clearly, ending in the cry that she had let out on falling.

At the moment when Pajadou had come crashing down beside her, it seemed to her that she had lost her footing, that she had fallen from a vertiginous height. And the back of the wagon vanished out of sight like a blank slate, like a treacherous trap door.

A voice rose from the courtyard.

"Go then and wake the little girl up!"

Pajadou cried out: "I'll go!"

So Reine shot up out of bed and dressed quickly, her hands feeling clumsy. A modesty had been awoken in her, and, suddenly, it struck her that she should not let him find her in bed, half naked...

When he entered, she was dressed, standing.

"There you are! You're awake?" he said.

She responded: "Yes, monsieur."

"Cut out the 'monsieur,' bit" he murmured. He took her into his arms, kissed her hair. He whispered into her ear: "Be quiet, don't say anything stupid, alright?"

They went downstairs.

At the bottom of the stairs, Reine met the boss lady and didn't dare raise her eyes, for fear that she would read her fault there. An uncomfortableness paralyzed her most natural movements; she felt ashamed walking in front of anyone. It seemed to her that someone ought to notice in her bearing, in the awkwardness of her dangling arms, something unusual or unnatural, she didn't know what, that wasn't there the day before. And she went forward, with precipitous steps, envying the women whose long dresses hid their feet. When a female worker kidded her on the thinness of her legs, she turned purple. Now, innocent words, everyday remarks, left her confused, brought blood to her cheeks. At home, fortunately, one went to bed after dinner, a brief meal during which few words were spoken. She was able to avoid then the looks that searched your face to punctuate an interrogation. For several days she felt an extreme embarrassment among the female workers. She was surprised to discover herself jealous of their strength, their healthy exertion, and that beautiful indifference that made them accept a man like a drudgery more annoying than others, – by habit or by self-interest. There were things she caught a glimpse of, unnamed things that she ardently desired to understand better; conversations among the girls that made her daydream for hours, a tension in her mind searching for hidden meaning in phrases, lifting the veil from the words, slowly, coupled at the same time with desire and apprehension, joy and the fear of seeing the innuendo she sought vanish, like smoke, into thin air, without giving up its secret. She discovered a profoundness in their silly questions, an occult meaning in their preposterous responses. She waited with fear alternating with impatience for the day when, once again, she would have to accompany Pajadou to Paris. She would have wanted a pretext, an illness, to keep her at Cachau, and she felt tears welling in her eyes at the thought that her lover would not bring her along.

He brought her along with him on Friday, then Monday, then all the Fridays and Mondays that followed. Reine slipped into vice imperceptibly, with more curiosity than pleasure. She suffered Pajadou with the idea that knowledge of a man hastened the development of her barely formed body, would make it like the girls' whose hips swayed freely.

She stood now for long minutes before the mirror, looking at her growing breasts...

"You look a little peaky," her mother said, "they aren't overworking you are they? No? It's a growth spurt, then!"

She wasn't growing any taller, however.

"Stand up straight," Madame Carniche continued, "you're slouching your back."

The truth was that Reine was pushing her shoulders back, thinking, in all conscience, to give herself stature thereby. She lived, since her descent, in a torpor, a state of drowsiness, a lax sluggishness that pulled her into vice, into joyless excesses, on a daily basis. But, in the shame of that monstrous coupling, she retained a profound respect, almost gratitude, for Pajadou. She loved him a little as a dog loves its master, the dispenser of joys and the supreme executor of justice. He had over her, besides the ascendent of a man who knows all about the woman who wants to learn, the authority of the boss over the apprentice, an authority that prevailed over all considerations. Also, logically, what attached her to Pajadou, outside the bindings of the flesh, had to lower her before Héloïse, to infuse her with a servant's humility. She found, in the situation she had now with respect to her patroness, the occasion to affirm her devotion and her respect where a pre-eminent bitch, a Léontine, would have only seen a level playing field, a familiarity or nearness that her concubinage with Pajadou established been her and Héloïse.

The laundress, tacitly okay with the child, and, moreover, made circumspect by the scenes that reminded her of his last love affairs, treated Reine, at the laundry, like a child, the baby, as the female workers called her. They seemed absolute strangers to one another.

One Monday, Pajadou left his wife in the middle of the night to go find Reine in her room. Héloïse, getting up at four in the morning, was surprised not to see her husband in bed, but, as she was opening the window, she noticed him smoking in the courtyard.

Never has he gotten up so early before, she thought.

And she brought it up with him.

"Colic," he said.

XIII

It was the following Monday, toward eight o'clock.

"Madame Pajadou, there's someone downstairs wants to talk with you."

Héloïse descended. Pavanne removed his cap, looked around. Nobody being in earshot, he began:

"Here's the deal. I was sent by Léontine. She had her lil one last Thursday. She was hoping to return to work this week, but appears, by what the doctor says, there's a complication, I don't know what... So she is without resources, you understand?... Not a *sou*!"

Héloïse looked at him, mistrustful.

Pavanne lowered his voice: "I didn't ask the bossman, 'cause..."

Héloïse gave him twenty francs.

"For reals, this ain't a joke," concluded Pavanne, putting the money in his pocket; "also she told me to leave you her address so you could come see her, my poor neighbor. She doesn't want you to think these are tall stories."

He gave her a scrap of paper and exited while walking backwards, bidding her adieu.

XIV

Reine and Pajadou returned. She got down out of the wagon, entered the dining room and deposited on the corner of the buffet a package she was holding in her hand. But Pajadou, who was unharnessing the horse, called Reine, invited her to come back and help him.

Héloïse, who was setting the table, took the package and untied it without thinking. It contained a little girl's rolled pair of pants.

Reine came back in.

"Is this yours?" asked Héloïse, pointing to the package, where the child had left it and which she had wrapped back up.

"Yes, madame," responded Reine, having turned quite red in the face suddenly.

Two days later, during Pajadou's absence,

Mother Vaillant, from a window of the room where Reine slept every Monday night, called out to Héloïse, who was walking across the courtyard.

"Héloïse! Wasn't your husband asking you this morning about a cuff button he'd lost?"

"Yeah."

"Well, maybe this is it." She threw the bone button into the apron that Héloïse held out for her.

"That's the one," said Héloïse.

"Well, I found it under the lil one's bed, while sweeping."

Héloïse, seized suddenly, leaned against the wall, and she felt a sharp pain in her chest that forced a small cry from her. Brusquely, three dark clouds that were, at that moment, barely three black spots on the horizon, clambered forward, jostled each other, joined and burst over her head. A minute later, she saw Pajadou smoking in the courtyard again, at four in the morning; she saw Reine looking confused while picking up her package off the buffet; and she saw Mother Vaillant discovering the button under the apprentice's bed. These three incidents which, in appearance, had no connection, suddenly rose up in her mind, filled it entirely, like the last argument of an indictment, gathering in one phrase all the charges leveled against the accused, shedding light on them skillfully in such a way that they logically and implacably led to a condemnation.

"Where are you going?" Mother Vaillant

asked Héloïse, who was leaving.

"To go speak with them," she responded with feigned indifference. But as her children wanted to follow her, she ordered them to wait for her at the door of the laundry. It was nine thirty at night. The lights were pale on the ground floor of the buildings where ironers were working late and behind the glass windows of the boutiques where drinkers were laughing, sitting at tables. She exited the wide street and entered rue des Deux Parcs, at the end of which she found the avenue de Cachau. Both these streets were absolutely deserted, the first was bordered on the right and left by the enclosing walls of two parks that gave it its name; the avenue grew larger between the two rows of dark houses that parted, on the right, at the height of the railroad bridge, to reveal, barring the horizon, the dark mass of the aqueduct with its tall arcades. As she passed under the bridge, a deafening rumbling sound shook it, and one instant later the train, coming from Sceaux, arrived at the Arcueil-Cachau station, which she left at the right. Then Héloïse began to run, all alone in the night, breathing heavily. She reached the route d'Orleans and descended towards the gate. Shivers ran through her body, and a strong desire to cry gripped her throat, and shook her chest since morning. Her teeth chattered, although beads of sweat, large like tears, ran down the length of her nostrils to her lips. A sound of bells stopped her dead in her tracks. She recognized their wagon, which held the middle of the road and wasn't yet but a big black dot in the moonless night. She stepped off the sidewalk, went in front of the wagon, craning her neck with circumspection.

The horse, its reins dangling over its croup, advanced at a pace equal to the swinging of its head and chest in a rocking rhythm. Behind it, on the seat, nobody was seated... Héloïse had a desire to jump at the head of the horse, climb up onto the step, and look inside the wagon... She was seized with a rage to kill them by blows with her heels, to pummel them to death with her fists, to push their faces down, stick their noses into the mud... Then, nearly out of her mind, she let the wagon pass, caught onto the back of it. She whipped up her grief, intensified it, made it drunk on the sighs that she heard on the other side of the thin partition that separated her from the two lovers!

But Pajadou was already on the seat of the wagon. "Some kid again," he said.

He leaned outside the wagon and launched a great volley of strokes with the whip...

A groaning sound broke the silence, and, in the night, a body came crashing down on its knees behind the wagon.

Pajadou shouted: "Take that, you rascal!"

XV

That was the beginning of Héloïse's painful and slow climb up Calvary: her climb with its stations where she bruised her knees, with the collapsing of her body under the weight of the cross, and the trepidations of her eyelids in the lacrimose face. But the first station was marked by a revulsion of the offended flesh, of the bleeding heart!

Several minutes after Pajadou's arrival at the laundry, Héloïse returned in turn, her fingers bruised by the blows of the whip, her face and hair full of dirt.

Dinner was filled with silence; but when the little one left the table, Héloïse, with a resolute authority that her mother didn't recognize in her, said to the old laundress, while indicating Pajadou with a gesture: "Leave us; we have something to speak about."

He lifted his head as Mother Vaillant took her leave. Then they remained face to face, with the cleared table between them. Héloïse led the attack resolutely, head on. For her it was a decisive battle, her all-or-nothing. She felt filled with an extraordinary energy. She had dragged herself home, speaking to herself in the dark, her teeth clenched, with large menacing gestures. He would respond like this, by golly! Or even like that... In a word, she nailed him to the pillory, crushed, dribbling, vanquished!

She got up from the table and, straight to it, threw these words into his face: "I know everything! You are sleeping with the little one!"

He didn't deny it, kept his magnificent cool, and said simply:

"And then?"

"And then!..." She grabbed the bottle of brandy that was resting on the table by the neck, and she brandished it... Then, suddenly calmed, she sat back down:

"This is stupid, all this, let's talk. Don't lie! You love the child? No, that's not possible; you satisfy your dirty desires with her as you would do with the first girl that came along... That's fine, because you have that one under your thumb; it's more convenient. Don't tell me no... I know!"

He sniggered, which enraged her.

"So, it's children now, huh! There aren't enough cows walking the sidewalks. Orgies in the city don't cut it anymore; you pick up thirteen-year-old girls now because you're tired of those filth who fling their sickness at you! Now you need children who don't know what's what? You're a dog!"

She put both her hands on the table, her bust leaning towards him and, lowering her voice, she added:

"Do you want me to tell you where your dirty haymaking will lead you? To the penal colony!"

"Do you intend to denounce me?" asked Pajadou.

She stammered: "I want... I want you to leave her alone, or I will throw her out."

He said calmly: "I will follow her."

"I will tell her parents."

"I will abduct her."

"She won't follow you..."

"She will follow me," he responded cooly, full of confidence, and each reply of his was a crack of the whip that elicited a muted cry from Héloïse.

She softened her voice, sought a tender tone of voice.

He had children, little ones too... Let's see, if, instead of raising boys, they raised girls and someone came to take one of them off their hands at fourteen years old, defiled her, what would he say? Was that love at that age?

He hummed a tune:

> *There are loves at every age*
> *And flowers...*

But she got up, and he changed his tune.

"When you say: 'I have it, I will keep it!'..."

That cynical joke of his riled Héloïse's weak flesh; shuddering, she ran to the door and blurted this out again: "I will report you! I will tell everything... I will have it corroborated by a doctor... everything!"

He grabbed her, but she struggled, without crying out, while pounding her head against his bosom, while he tried to hold on to her by her wrists. When his scratched chest bled beneath his shredded undershirt, he held her two hands crushed in his own, then he murmured mechanically:

"Report it if you want, we'll see! Ah! as far as that goes, don't you know then that everyone will be against you; men, women... everyone! They will say it's a scheme, an invention by your mother to chase me outta here, because I took her place! And the doctor, let him come! The little girl's virginity has been taken, and then what? She'll confess a lover, a Pierre or a Paul. Go look for him. Not seen, not heard!... An inquest? Well! So be it, I will be arrested, condemned, screwed! And your children, – have you thought this through? The kids of a convict, I do believe!"

He pushed her away: "You won't report it, will you? No. So don't play nasty, or I will leave tomorrow and take Reine with me; and you won't see us again."

She wept now and said: "To the very end, what do you reproach me with?"

He responded: "Do you think I enjoy being with you? For five years, I have had to take possession, step by step, minute by minute, of your business, after your mother treated me like a robber. Today I'm the boss, I will have my fun!"

"Fine," continued Héloïse, "but there are women for that, to amuse yourself. Have I ever, when you took your mistresses from among the women of the laundry, – have I ever reproached you for it? But this little girl! One day, the truth will out. She has parents: it's forced labor for you!"

He got up, visibly annoyed, "Are you done?"

She shouted loudly, "No!"

He opened the door: "Then I will go join her!"

But Héloïse had gone out ahead of him; she crossed the courtyard and went up to go find Reine in her room, above the workshop, while Pajadou, who simply desired that the scene should come to an end, went back to the eating room.

Sure enough, the little girl had been on pins and needles since the meal! For, although she had returned to her room over half an hour earlier, she had only lain down on her bed and had not yet blown out the candle when Héloïse entered.

She went straight to the child's bed, acting very gentle all of the sudden, for fear she might frighten the child and give Pajadou the opportunity to intervene.

"Reine, you must leave," she said, "I cannot keep you any longer."

"M'sieu Pajadou will not want..."

"But don't you realize that if someone caught you two together... yes, I know everything, – he will go to prison?"

"Why?"

Suddenly, Héloïse was disarmed by that naïvety, that child's questioning, the kind that leaves mothers perplexed; looking for a small way out. Héloïse searched for the words to deal with that still chaste, deflowered modesty. Why? Because she was just a little girl. Couldn't they keep it secret; besides, if they hadn't done anything wrong?...

That argument struck her. So Reine had never dreaded this catastrophe: that their lovemaking would be found out. Pajadou had groomed her by design with this ignorant peace of mind.

Clearly, she had never noticed the effort he had taken to avoid, before strangers, any word, any petting, in which a misunderstanding could have taken root; but they were, on that point, tacitly in agreement, and, one on one, Pajadou had never so much as hinted that an imprudence on their part could have doomed them. My goodness! Yes, she knew quite well that their conduct was unacceptable, given they made love in the wagon, while making the rounds; but was it really true that their mistake made Pajadou liable to go to prison? Now she had her doubts; a shift was happening in her mind. She suspected a trap that the boss lady was setting for her to take her husband violently away from her. And she sobbed, seized despite everything by that threat: prison, but divided, fundamentally, between a fear of gendarmes and the idea of a brazen machination on the part of Héloïse.

This latter was more disarmed, more vanquished by the little girl's tears and sobs than by her husband's cynicism and brutality.

She sat down on the bed at Reine's feet:

"Okay, promise me you will leave, that you will go back to your parents."

Héloïse, without knowing it, had just touched the nerve. The child's despair burst out: Her father would beat her: she would rather die!

"Then we will not send you back," continued the laundress; "we will find another place for you."

Reine moaned.

"M'sieu Pajadou told me he would go wherever I go."

"You poor little girl! If your father found out, however..."

"He would kill me..."

"There you go."

"Oh! but M'sieu Pajadou said that we would save ourselves, that we would hide somewhere, far-away, and that he would protect me."

"You would go with him then?"

"Yes, Madame."

"You love him then?"

"Yes, Madame."

But there was, in the second response, murmured with moist eyes, more fear than love. All of a sudden, Héloïse understood that Pajadou dominated his mistress just as he had subjugated her, his wife! She understood that he would leave like he said he would, in the event their love affair would out.

Reine rolled herself up into a ball under the sheets, crying into her pillow. She said: "I promise I will be good, work hard... but don't send me away; at home I would tell everything, then my father would kill me!..."

"But you would go with him, however..."

"It's M'sieu Pajadou who wants it, I swear to you, Madame!... me, it makes me ill!..."

Héloïse was affected by those tears, she understood now that the child had succumbed, pushed into evil by an irresistible force. Reine inspired an immense pity in her, not hatred; it pained her to see this young girl in the arms of her husband, because she felt that he didn't love his new mistress anymore than he loved the previous ones. His wife, her too? She had been the glorious mistress, the trophy wife that one shows off and by whom one arrives, that's all! She felt a revulsion in her honest and upright nature at the thought that that miserable forty-five-year-old man, whose name she had taken, debauched fourteen-year-olds, not quite women, whose naïvety continued to poke its head out however from beneath all the filth!

The candle went out and, suddenly, the room became dark...

Reine was still sobbing in her sheets. A huge fear seized her when the darkness fell all around her. She thought that the boss lady was going to take advantage of the obscurity to leap at her throat and strangle her, trample her underfoot furiously! And she felt that she would not even have enough strength to cry out!

But Héloïse sat there immobile, at the foot of the bed, her elbows on her knees, and her chin in her hands.

Now the very large sheets that were drying at the far end of the room seemed like the very tall walls of a prison. The cord from which the sheets hung looked like the crest of the wall, and above it, shadows passed, grimacing!... then the doors opened...

A gust of wind pushed open the window that was poorly shut; so that the sheets shivered, and the walls, like the walls on a stage being pushed into the wings, moved. The dance of hanging linen started all over again!

Reine, beside herself with fear, didn't want to fall asleep. Héloïse, she thought, was waiting for that moment to strangle her! But a breeze from outside was freezing cold to her. She snuggled up under the covers, slowly slid into a sleep, and finished by abandoning herself to it, overcome and tired of fighting, having made the sacrifice of her life!

Throughout the night, Héloïse watched over the child, sleeping, without thinking to close the window by which the wind entered and blew on them.

XVI

Life became intolerable. In six weeks time, Héloïse and her mother aged ten years.

Mother Vaillant in particular was unrecognizable. Her soft, drooping cheeks seemed to melt; the poor woman was dissolving into bile. The only sign of life in her face was her eyes, her feverish eyes

grown larger and more deep-set. Reine had her constantly in hot pursuit. She moved through the hall-
ways, exercised over the child a stubborn surveillance. But with her body's corpulence, her good
health and strength had left her. She now had to gasp
for air, experienced heavy breathing, let out wheezing
sounds like an old, overworked machine. As she barely left her room, except to follow Reine, she remained
for entire days in her camisole, without corset, her bosom loose, her breasts bouncing. She was a disaster.
Héloïse, on the other hand, as at the time of her first
sorrows, threw herself, head down, into her work with
a vengeance, accepting, even seeking out, the harshest
drudgery that would dull her thoughts. She was out of
bed at four o'clock in the morning, and she was the
last person to retire at night. She folded all the packets, washed, ironed. without a moment's rest, without
a complaint! She exerted herself in useless and crush-
ing tasks more fit for a beast of burden, without realizing the mistake she was doing to her business, on a
whole, without noticing that the laundry, deprived of
intelligent direction, was going downhill.

Constant dissatisfaction sent the clients to
Cachau; delays in returning their linen provoked
wrathful complaints. Then the creditors showed up
without warning, and, hitting a wall of perfect indifference with the boss, they went to find the two wom-
en. Mother Vaillant nearly died of a heart attack the
first time she was approached for a contracted debt
incurred by the son-in-law.

She made a terrible scene with Pajadou, re-
traced the history of the business that Monsieur Vail-

lant had established, recounted the hesitations, the first struggles, the energy expended to put the laundry on a sound footing!... In the end, she threw the dead-man into her son-in-law's face, like the prototype of commercial probity, the man who never owed a *sou*! And she played the cadaver, used it like an offensive weapon, to knock Pajadou out!

Nowadays he spent his time at the cafe. It was there that he found people whose confidence he wanted to gain and naïve people or flatterers whose lot he pitied. In the evening, between two games of billiards, he didn't hold back. He talked about the last two scenes that his wife and his mother-in-law had made and he added, like a good boy, that "that didn't prevent him from loving them!" He pretended to forgive the one, – her change in life which tormented her, he believed; and the other, – her claim to rights that she had never abdicated. The thurst of the matter thus displaced, – he arrived at the cafe shattered, rallied the drinkers to his side by his resigned sadness, and his silent despondency. Little by little, he grew more animated. He had even been forced to move out! They were making his life unbearable!

The shaking of hands, the banalities that exhorted him to have patience, the sought-after pity seemed to mollify him. He sat down in the corner, but someone had need of an opponent at billiards or a fourth at piquet; he got up, played, always lost and paid for the drinks with a good grace that won everyone's heart!

It was all an act, for the two women had spared him their reproaches since the scene that

Héloïse had made about Reine. Only at mealtime did they get together, reunited around the same table, Mondays and Fridays, his legitimate wife and his mistress. Both of them suffered equally. Reine had at first refused to accompany Pajadou on his rounds, but he lost his temper, shouted that she could leave... Then she saw herself, returning to her parents, between the impassive and severe Carniche and her mother, with her gentle, but monotonous sadness; she went over her life in her mind, between her father, who would beat her, and the poor woman, who had nothing to defend her with but her furtive tears and fearful caresses, – and that existence in perspective made her think of suicide. She made plans, then abandoned them; finally she sank back down into a life of joyless vice and bestial debauchery.

She now had downcast eyes, a leaden taint to her complexion from the fatigues of the flesh, and an insomnia haunted by genii with the heads of gendarmes. She always started by refusing Pajadou with a growing terror, an apprehension he could not vanquish. She acceded to him finally, but with what mad fears? He was exasperated with her, even though possession of her had a greater charm, thus whipped up by the refusals, the obstacles that stimulated his desire, over and over again.

Two or three times, her father, Carniche, passed by the laundry, asked Héloïse if she was satisfied with Reine.

Héloïse responded: But of course... And she covered her mouth with her hands, so as not to cry out loud: Take her back! Don't you see that you are killing her? How long can we keep dragging this shame behind us?

She was arrested also by the fear of a scandal that sent the father of her children to prison.

Then again, that little girl had with her, by nature, more than one affinity. Héloïse saw herself in that little girl whose spinelessness of spirit, a stupid need for humble submission, chased her into Pajadou's arms. She was filled with commiseration, and she had been on the verge of complaining about that apprentice whose father said: "Mamma Pajadou, if you are not satisfied with her, send her back to me; I will take it on myself to teach her to enjoy work!"

Héloïse, moreover, worried her mother, Madame Vaillant. To the excessive activity that she had expended to deaden her grief, unsuccessfully, succeeded a physical feebleness that together with a natural, moral torpor, contributed to the morbid state of her two systems. Héloïse remained for hours on end, her mouth open, in a chair. She fell asleep standing, at the table, walking, everywhere. She rose in the morning with a lassitude resulting from a sort of hypnophobia similar to that which peopled Reine's dreams, with prisoners dragging their chains, and solemn phantoms, with their luminous, dancing eyes!

Often, at night, she went downstairs, in a nightshirt, into the courtyard, and opened the door to imaginary beings that she greeted with the low bows of a little girl. When she didn't run away, frightened out of her mind by the gleam of naked sabers or the vague shadow that fantastic cocked hats[1] cast against the wall, she stopped dead in her tracks, filled with that peace that falls from heaven. In the street, the poles of the laundries grew longer, seemed to extend out of the shadow of the windows with a menacing stiffness, and let hang in right folds, like the folds of a winding sheet, the very white and disproportionately long sheets that a light breeze swelled.

An invisible crowd teemed, clamored, howled... Then Héloïse went back inside, seeing off the visitors she had let in, and regaining her bed with tranquil step. Pajadou was afraid and locked himself in his room. For some time, moreover, he didn't sleep in the same room with his wife, having scruples about leaving the conjugal bed to rejoin his mistress, under Héloïse's eyes, who, on those nights, inserted pins into her thighs in order to combat sleep.

And they no longer lived, summoning a decisive crisis with all their soul, one of those crises impatiently expected, that saves the patient or damns him irremediably!

XVII

At this juncture, Léontine showed up at the laundry. She had placed her baby with a wet nurse in Rueil, but the wet nurse required the first month's payment immediately. Léontine asked for an advance of money which the laundress gave to her. As for taking her back, she hesitated. But Mother Vaillant had a bril-

---

[1] cocked hats: the kind that gendarmes wore.

liant idea. Who knows? Pajadou could perhaps get back together with that girl; they drew up a comparison between the two girls to Léontine's advantage, between the latter's fullness of shape, her tempting flesh of a well-endowed woman, and Reine's spindly body and thin legs. The incident, after all, hadn't compromised anyone who wasn't already compromised. Héloïse came around to welcoming with a secret joy the return to the laundry of an old mistress of her husband's. He needed a woman! They threw that one at him, – like a bone already gnawed on that he ought to return to and sniff at, if not to take up in his gob again.

Héloïse, however, counted on some resistance, comments, a complete comedy which she would not have been the dupe of, but which, given the man's Jesuitism, would have assured the trick's success. She was disappointed. If Pajadou thought at all about Léontine's return, he didn't show it. His passion for Reine was growing, excited as it was by the little girl's terrors, who refused rendez-vous, but gave in with a thousand reticences. He had to renounce the visits he paid her when she was sleeping at the laundry. Those visits threw her into a panic; behind her lover were Héloïse and her mother bringing the police with them!

Then Pajadou wouldn't let himself be concerned by the frequency and acuteness of arthritic pains he had been suffering for two years now.

Out of the blue, an articular rheumatism confined him to bed. His cries, his swearing, echoed throughout the house. An irritable humor caused by the malady made him insupportable. He wanted to see Reine every day, imaging that they would take advantage of the boss' absence to send her away. Two or three times Léontine walked through Pajadou's room. He looked at her without surprise, without recognizing her.

XVIII

Pajadou said at the end of the doctor's visit: "I will get out of bed tomorrow." He was no longer suffering, grew strapping again, stirred in his bed by desires, by a formidable convalescent appetite. The sensual desire of the male for the female sex was also reborn with all its ardors, its lusts, an immense need to expend again its forces, which the rheumatism had neutralized. Léontine had come again asking for an advance. Every Saturday, it was the same song. The baby had need of clothing, the baby required this, the wet nurse that; the infant was growing poorly, it was difficult to raise, no matter, she didn't regret a thing, etc.... It was a perfectly planned blackmail, for the child having been stillborn, all the money went to Pavanne, who lived the fat life and no longer needed to resort to three-card tricks to play out his roguish fantasies. But he made a tactical mistake by coming to hang around the laundry, and suddenly Héloïse smelled a rat. Léontine did her best to convince her that Pavanne was an old neighbor who came to give her news of the baby, but Héloïse flat out refused her latest request for an advance. The girl didn't insist, but she promised herself to consult with her lover and get his advice. He concluded that the boss lady no longer had enough to give them and that Léontine needed to tap the boss.

Héloïse, for her part, approached Pajadou; strong enough now so that a clear and frank explanation wouldn't fatigue him. He was sitting on his bed. Héloïse closed the door and told him her story straight off. She confessed to the advances given to Léontine; Pajadou interrupted her often: "You're stupid," he said, "never money, never! Have you seen the kid? They're pulling the wool over your eyes!" Then he became very gentle, measured his words, surprised his wife who was expecting his reproaches, a violent outburst where he threw all the mistakes into her face, in order to make her forget that he was, he alone, the cause of these disorders.

When she had said all she had to say, he took her hands, looked into her eyes, ardently, with a sudden desire that lit up his face and displayed some saliva on his lips. She recoiled, but he was holding her by the wrists, and, fallen over to the side, was pulling her towards him, inviting her with his eyes to lie down next to him. – She refused, sickened, repugnant to the sort of commerce that she had lost the habit of and that, besides, had only left her disgusted. Pajadou lost his temper however and, without letting her go, cried out: "I want it!... I want it!..." She responded: "No!" freed her bruised arms and, with a bound, gained the extremity of the room, decided to threw herself down the stairs if he was going to force her.

He got up, strong in the legs, taken by a blinding rage. He repeated: "You don't want it? Be careful what you say! You don't want it?" She said "no" with a movement of her head. So he got dressed, fumbling with his hands because he was blinded with anger, and a desire to beat her until he was satisfied.

She thought he was going to throw himself at her, take her by force, but, without saying a word, pushing her aside with a brutal movement, he passed in front of her, opened the door, and went downstairs into the courtyard.

Night had fallen; all the workers had gone home. Pajadou shouted: "Reine!"

Léontine, who had lingered behind, stopped to tell him that the child had left the laundry.

Pajadou looked out of sorts; then, after a moment of reflection, he accosted his old mistress, and they exhibited the attitude and the facial expressions of two crafty characters who were working out the details of a transaction. In the end, he got the better of the girl's feigned or real hesitations. Bah! He knew quite well that the story of her child was a trick; it didn't matter to him, he would give her the money that his wife had refused her.

Léontine didn't depart.

At dinnertime, Héloïse didn't go downstairs at all, fearing an explanation before her mother. She went to bed early, pretexting a migraine. But she was still not asleep when, around ten o'clock, Pajadou entered the room. Héloïse didn't understand at first why Léontine was with him. He closed the door when she crossed the threshold, and, without appearing to notice the presence of his wife, he told the worker:

"Take off your clothes!...."

Héloïse sat up in bed immediately, red in the face, revulted. She cried out: "You want..." but she lost her voice; a stupor riveted her to the bed. Léontine herself, despite the girl's swagger and all her dismissive rancor, hesitated, stood motionless with her arms dangling, with a stupid look on her face.

Pajadou said it again: "Take off your clothes." He had a false laugh: "Do you hear? I have a wife who will not sleep with me; in other words, I'm hungry and I cannot find anything to eat in the house. As I don't want to go outside, someone needs to bring me my dinner from the outside, no?" A look of malicious joy suffused his face, then the girl, planted in the middle of the room, made him impatient... Brutally, he uncovered her breasts, pulled the clips and pins out of her hair which fell, thick and pomaded, over her shoulders.

Léontine murmured: "Oh well, never mind!" and her skirts dropped to the floor.

Héloïse jumped to the foot of the bed, and threw herself at her, but Pajadou interposed himself, without losing his cool, spurred on by a cold cockiness that exasperated. He took his wife by the wrists and said straight to her face: "That offends you, my chaste one? Why do you get up? Isn't the bed big enough for the three of us?"

A hissing sound in his throat made him change his tone of voice: he continued: "I told you! You wanted it, besides; was it me who let Léontine return to the laundry? Now, stay or go, but leave us be!"

He saw the girl in her chemise, her naked feet on the bedside rug; then he added: "Get into bed then! I will be with you shortly; the time to escort madame!"

But Héloïse blew up in his face, spitting on the bed, where her worker was taking her place which was still warm. In the fight that ensued, her nightshirt slipped and her thin shoulders and her flat chest were exposed, exaggerating the cavity of her clavicles, two pits the size of a baby's fist. She resisted, slipped out of Pajadou's fingers, bounded towards the bed with her scratches and terrible biting. This only prolonged the game; he took pleasure in that contact with warm flesh leaving the sheets, in rubbing up against that nudity smelling good and whetting his appetite. It was the hors-d'oeuvre before a choice dish that the girl wallowing on the bed was going to serve him.

Never had he seen his wife in such a state of overexcitement; she foamed at the mouth, her mouth twisted, her eyes leaving the sockets. The insults that exited her lips, groaned, died, turned into crazy gestures. And that strangulation of cries that she had wanted to let out, plus Pajadou's mutism, who contented himself with paring her blows, and the stupor of that girl who watched, reduced the sound of the struggle to a stifled stamping, a muted heaving.

But it had to stop. Pajadou seized Héloïse with both hands, carried her, pushed her into the stairway, slamming the door on her. Bolted it.

Héloïse found herself in the courtyard, out of her mind, crazy. Then it was, throughout the house, like a beast let loose, galloping. In her nightshirt, her hair undone, she went through all the rooms on the ground floor. Sometimes, in a hallway, she stopped before a door, placed her ear to the keyhole and ran away. Drops of sweat collected on her skin, and she made extraordinary efforts to cry out loud, but she could not unclench her teeth; she had a lump in her throat, which she kneaded with both hands, furiously! In the room where Reine slept on Mondays, she stopped short before the empty bed! She destroyed it, with a furious trampling of her feet, pulled the stuffing out of the mattress, which she bit, her mouth full of horse hair! In the rooms where the linen dried on cords, the sheets whipped her face, a freshness sent shivers up and down her moist skin. Then having crossed through the workshop, an exterior door pushed open, she found herself in front of the Bièvre[2], which flowed a small ways beneath the laundry. Boards supported by posts created, above the course of the water, a kind of promontory, where the sabots of one of the women, who wet the linen before placing it in the wash box, had been left behind. Héloïse lost her footing and fell onto her knees. All of a sudden, an extremely cold sensation gripped her, and a fine little drizzle like a fog froze her to the marrow. Silence reigned; the countryside, on the other side of the Bièvre, stretched out sad and bare, striped by a row of meager trees, with leaves on top that seemed like long feather dusters the earth had pushed up to-

---

[2] Bièvre: the name of a river in Île-de-France that flows into the Seine.

wards a vast ceiling of heavy and black clouds. A dog
was heard howling in the distance. There was a deep
wailing, a prolonged sobbing by a child who was suffering. Héloïse listened, her head leaning to one
side... But a feeling of fear shook her, and she vaguely understood that her feet were standing in a pool of
water. A coolness penetrated her, ran under her skin,
from the nape of her neck down to her heels.

An intoxicated voice, the sound of a man who
beats on the walls, was heard.

The voice belted out the first verse of an inept
refrain:

There's no umbrella...

And, suddenly, the dog's distant plaint became heartrending, hiccoughing at times, then stri-
dent, ringing out into the night like a desperate plea,
the clarion notes of a supreme chiming!

The voice completed the refrain, as it grew
more distant:

He's wet to the bones!...

And, straightaway, as if in accompaniment
with the drunkard, the sky cracked. The rain pattered
onto the surface of the Bièvre, beat on the window
panes, sang its crisp song in the peace of the night.
The dog fell silent... Then, as if the howling had put a
spell on Héloïse that the faint rain broke, the laundress picked herself up again, her nightshirt clinging
to her wet body. But as she was returning to the
house, a pipe burst above her head, covering her in

dirty water that giggled behind her back with the lap-
ping sound of a waterfall.

When Mother Vaillant rose the following
morning, she found Héloïse, curled up in a ball, huddled up against her door, half-naked and sleeping!

XIX

She was found to have a fever, the delirium never left
the poor woman again. Mother Vaillant never left her
bedside; Pajadou stayed away from the patient's door
for fear that Héloïse's incoherent babbling would
make him look bad. Visitors, in any case, were rare,
given that the two women didn't associate with their
neighbors. To the people who, in passing, felt obliged
to ask for news of Héloïse, Pajadou responded:
"Don't talk to me about it! The devil if I know how
she got that chill and fever; the doctor is hopeful he
can save her!" The room in which he holed himself
up was adjacent the room where Héloïse was confined to bed. He received visitors with a serious attitude, and a tearful voice of contained emotion, speaking softly. Ah! He would be beside himself if adversi-
ty should take his wife away from him. He hadn't
spent twelve years with her without having grown attached by other bonds than those of the flesh!

Friends who had been touched by his café
comedy act ventured discreet allusions to the scenes
that cast a shadow over their marriage.

They said, as if Héloïse no longer left in their
minds anything but the memory of an ancient death:

"Is it not the case that she was a bit... cantankerous?"

Pajadou nodded his head. Well, yes, he hadn't always been very happy, but that meant nothing... he missed her all the same. For him, as for all his friends, his wife had lived; their phrases buried her, each word that fell from their lips was a shovelful of earth thrown into the open grave. When the doctor had given up on Héloïse, Pajadou had decided to hire someone to assist Mother Vaillant watch Héloïse: a neighbor woman who had offered her services.

Maman Lapoint was a small, old, deaf woman, who lived on a rental income that one of her brothers had gifted her with in the countryside. She had never had, never avowed at any rate, but two passions in life: the theater when she was young; and reading, ever since her deafness made theater halls pointless. She consumed a frightful number of novels, took head on four serialized novels at a time, published by small journals, and ransacked the so-called literary bookstores.

She arrived every morning at Pajadou's, with, in her arms, a batch of terrible stories cut by complaisant hands from the bottom tier of rags for a *sou*. She sat down in front of the bed, never interrupting her reading except to tell a chaplet of extravagant remedies whose efficaciousness Dennery's[3] heroes had experienced. Héloïse's illness struck her, awakened in her a thousand memories. She went over all the cases of madness she had known about. She had

---

[3] Dennery's: Adolphe Philippe d'Ennery (1811-1899), a French dramatist and novelist.

seen, in her youth, the *The Grace of God*, *Marie-Jeanne*, the *The Fortune Teller*,[4] ten other dramas by celebrated conjurors able to pull the wool over one's eyes. Then, looking at Mother Vaillant from above her reading glasses, she said, while pointing at Héloïse, "The thing is, you see, she needs to be made to cry; if she cries she will be saved; it's just like I'm telling you!"

Only, she hesitated among the twenty methods that dramatic charlatanism placed at her disposal, enough to bring tears to a fool's eyes. There were more than enough bonging of bell towers or even the tinkling of bells in children's choirs. There were also chants by monks or nuns, the groaning of organs... but the most infallible method, in her opinion, was the unexpected return of a beloved person, absent after a long period of time.

"Let's see, Madame Vaillant, rack your brain. Do you not have in your family someone who might fit the bill? It's deplorable: some tears and she's saved!"

She lowered her head, absorbed in her reading of the *Ravin des Torrents*, full of contempt for Mother Vaillant, who was left cold by those housewife remedies or remedies of a dramaturge in quest of a denouement!

Héloïse did not recognize anyone anymore, and her mother, who did not leave her side, had difficulty herself unraveling the thread of ideas from the

---

[4] *The Grace of God, Jeanne-Marie, The Fortune Teller*: the first two are by d'Ennery, the third is by Victor Séjour (1817-1874).

constant flow of words she let out. They had to re-move from the wall two lithographs, "The Departure" and "The Return," in the style of ten-o'clock curfew painter Gérard.[5] Mother Vaillant believed that Héloïse saw first the Queen then Léontine in the figure of a girl hanged by the neck by the French guard. But the moribund let out blood-curdling cries when they tried, at the same time, to get rid of a framed religiose pic-ture: A synoptic image of Catholic religion. In an oval, communicants were kneeling, their hands joined, lifting their unctuous faces to look at the priest. Around them, on the edges, were smiling, winged heads, blossoming roses, and lilies and doves. The hearts of Jesus and the hearts of Mary seemed full of flaming tow. Next to the baptistery, where a woman, whose crinoline formed improbable haunch-es, was holding a child over the font, the altar rose. That was the moment when the communicants laid down, the length of the holy table, ideal whitenesses the color of incense smoke. But those virgins exasper-ated Héloïse after having first amused her. They re-moved the image.

Mother Vaillant had continual surprises. She made an effort to understand the words that her daughter spoke: umbrella... to the bone... recurring constantly in every possible way with a nodding of the head. Then Mother Vaillant held Héloïse in her arms, rocking her like a little child. She alone still conserved some illusory doubts as to the seriousness of the illness that was killing her daughter.

---

[5] Gérard: probably a reference to French painter and illustrator François Gérard (1770-1837).

"Musical expressions would do her a world of good." And Mother Vaillant imitated Madame Ledieu, trying to find the caresses and modulations of her flute-like voice again. She murmured, and interspersed trills and appoggiatura into her phrases, all those she could remember: "We all climb Calvary, my dear, each one carries his cross in this world... The good God will not abandon us, come on!..."

But her nature regained the upper hand; muffled, grumpy anger could be detected in her voice; then she calmed herself down again. She would mend, by God! They moved out of the house; they lived the two of them, with the children, in a small corner... One needed only to drink that... and then that too!...

The poor old woman went a little bonkers herself. She spoke to Héloïse, in the language of a little negress, children's nonsense and lovers' coo-coos, together with the hypnotizing songs of nannies, little kisses, mother's little smiles, teasing blows of air... She put their two heads together on the pillow, saying: "How good we are! Good little Loïse... will drink a tisane! We are big girls now, that one puts to bed early, because we must go *promprom* tomorrow..."

And she sang: "Sweet dreams, mademoiselle; who will take a little beddy-bye? it's the child with her mother!..."

But Héloïse, as soon as she was drowsy, bolted upright, stammered: "Umbrella!... umbrella!..." And Mother Vaillant collapsed, could not take it anymore, holding back the tears, biting her fists so as not to explode!...

Pajadou, who was listening from behind the door, heard a loud cry...

He thought: "That's it!" – and he opened the door halfway, gently.

His mother-in-law, overcome with tears, was sobbing on the breast of the deceased. Maman Lapointe, with a lost look on her face, went over it again in her mind – the fifth act of a melodrama... and a caress of violins in tremolo rocked her to sleep in an intimate and quiet beatitude.

XX

Carniche, from his doorsill, called out to Pajadou. "Come in then; we never see you anymore!" Pajadou walked back. The day laborer continued: "It's not the case that because you had to return the little one that you needs pass by without saying hallo. Goodness gracious! We are perfectly aware that the new laundress has her creatures. Ah what's going on these days?"

Pajadou told him that he had sold the house, keeping only the wagon and horse, which he had hired out to some drinking buddies. "My benefice is much thinner now and I'm calmer," he concluded.

"And the children?" asked Carniche.

"They live with their grandmother."

"They don't work yet?"

"They're still quite young!" said Pajadou.

"Ah, you see, if they grow accustomed to idleness, to *laziness*, it's all over! Oh! while the little one is here, I use her in the fabrication of nets... Only, I would prefer it if she had a job, you understand... But come inside for a moment..."

Night was falling. Pajadou could make out, in the shadows at the back of the room, Reine, seated, a shuttle between her hands, her eyes lowered and focused on her work. Before her, her mother, bent over, was pouring into a pan small balls of lead.

"Damn!" continued Reine's father, "she grows bored here, alone... The mother and me, we spend the whole day outside..."

He shook an enormous box, laid it down, turned it over, disappeared inside. In the end, he turned it upright again and asked flat out: "Don't suppose you could find something for the little one among your colleagues?... I don't dare ask... I'm afraid of overstepping..."

Pajadou, his back against the wall, reflected, seemed to come up with a scheme that might satisfy Carniche. Memories of recent past caused a great sense of well-being to descend over him; he had, on the surface of his skin, a light tingling sensation that aroused him like the caresses of a woman. Reine didn't raise her head, and he imagined more than he saw, dreaming also, ruminating over words and kisses.

He had a vague feeling that all he had to do was reach out his hand and take her again. Everything was giving her to him. The past, present boredom, a stupid job that cloistered her... So he dreamt of new loves, which the separation, broken chains, a recovered freedom, gave him the feeling of being young again. He still had some good years ahead of him... marriage for financial gain no longer tempted him, the idea of a calm happiness softened him... he took refuge in that love, savoring the delights of a rekindled relationship that was the crowning moment of his active life, the transitive passage from a middle age to old age.

Carniche interrogated him with his eyes, and his wife risked a short suspension of work, waiting for his response.

Pajadou, with a good-natured expression, spoke. He would see what he could do, it might work out. He even had a good family in mind... The little one would be fine... He would work out a scheme to have them let her go to Paris with him, which would distract her. Carniche nodded his hand: "Ah! thank you!" He sought a phrase that might be the exact expression of his thought, and he settled on this clumsy thing: "See what you can do, mouths that have no arms to nourish them by are useless mouths!... One must work!"

And he went furiously back to his box, making it pay dearly for the moment of respite he had given himself.

Pajadou departed...

Mother Carniche, who slid up behind him,

stopped him on the sill:

"Please, Mista Pajadou, find her a job with some good family, – she was so good with you all!"

Other Books by the Publisher

Fanchette's Pretty Little Foot
by Restif de La Bretonne

Je M'Accuse...
by Léon Bloy

My Hospitals & My Prisons
by Paul Verlaine

Salvation Through the Jews
by Léon Bloy

Words of a Demolitions Contractor
by Léon Bloy

Cellulely
by Paul Verlaine

Flowers of Bitumen
by Émile Goudeau

Songs for Her & Odes in Her Honor
by Paul Verlaine

On Huysmans' Tomb
by Léon Bloy

Ten Years a Bohemian
by Émile Goudeau

The Soul of Napoleon
by Léon Bloy

Other Books by the Publisher (cont.)

Blood of the Poor
by Léon Bloy

*Theresa the Philosopher &
The Carmelite Extern Nun*
by Marquis d'Argens &
Anne-Gabriel Meusnier de Querlon

A Platonic Love
by Paul Alexis

*Two Novellas: Francine Cloarec's Funeral
and Benjamin Rozes*
by Léon Hennique

*The Revealer of the Globe: Christopher Columbus
& His Future Beatification (Part One)*
by Léon Bloy

Joan of Arc and Germany
by Léon Bloy